Not Quite a Curse

Emily Martha Sorensen

Also by Emily Martha Sorensen

Standalones:
Black Magic Academy

Fairy Senses:
Fairy Eyeglasses
Fairy Compass
Fairy Earmuffs
Fairy Barometer
Fairy Pox
Fairy Slippers
Fairy Lunchbox
Fairy Icepack
Fairy Stopwatch
Fairy Toothbrush
Fairy Perfume

Dragon Eggs:
Dragon's Egg
Dragon's Hope
Dragon's First Christmas
Dragon's Fire

Comics:
A Magical Roommate
To Prevent World Peace

The End in the Beginning:
The Keeper and the Rulership
The Fires of the Rulership
The Magic or the Rulership

Trilogy of a Teenage Werevulture:
Trials of a Teenage Werevulture
Trifles of a Teenage Werevulture

The Numbers Just Keep
Getting Bigger:
Twenty-Four Potential
Children of Prophecy

Magical Mayhem:
To Prevent World Peace
To Prevent Chic Costumes
To Prevent Clear Paths
To Prevent Smart Choices
To Prevent Warm Welcomes

Short Story Collections:
Worlds of Wonder

Picture Books:
Tabby, Tabby, Burning Bright

http://www.emilymarthasorensen.com

To all the authors of shoujo manga
who have given me
loads of enjoyment over the years.

You know what inspired this book.

Chapter 1
Not Quite Aware

Lucy didn't realize she was cursed at first.

It wasn't like the day started out badly. In fact, it started out really well. For instance, there was the fact that she got asked out on three different dates by three different guys.

"Hey, Luce," George called, hurrying over as she shut her locker door. "Do you have any plans this Friday night?"

"Nope," Lucy said. "You?"

He grinned. "Well, I was hoping we might go out."

Lucy gave him an appraising look. She'd gone out with him a month ago. Too soon to go out with him again?

She'd found that when she went out with the same guy too many times in a row, he started to think they were going steady, and that just would not stand. She hated it when guys got clingy.

"Maybe," Lucy said, tossing her hair. "What time?"

"Dave's Pizza Buffet, right after school?" George asked. "We can double with one of your friends, if you want."

He knew her so well. Lucy loved double dates. They were so low-pressure.

Plus, then there would be *two* cute guys to stare at, rather than one. Her friends tended to have great taste in boys, too.

Not that, you know, she noticed or anything.

Anyway, at lunchtime, she passed by the really cute new boy who had just started school here a few days ago.

"Hi, Pablo," she said.

He did a double take, looking over at her. "Hi . . .?"

"Lucy," she said.

"You know my name," he said with surprise.

"I know everyone's names," she said matter-of-factly. She put no effort into schoolwork, but she had memorized the names of everybody at school. She liked saying hello to people, even the shy ones. Being popular didn't mean you had to be a jerk.

"Sorry I didn't know yours," he said.

"That's okay," she beamed. "You'd've heard it sooner or later. Everyone knows me. I'm the cutest girl in the school."

He stared at her.

"What?" she asked with a mischievous smile. "It's true. Should I be falsely modest?"

"Most people would."

"I'm not most people."

He laughed. "So I see."

"Well, I'd better get in line before the cafeteria runs out of anything good," she said, turning and waving. "Bye, Pablo."

"Wait!" he said. "I can't believe I'm asking this, but . . . do you have any plans this weekend?"

"Are you asking me out?" she asked with an impish grin.

"Am I asking out the cutest girl in the school? Well, it seems like a wise thing to do."

"Sure," Lucy said. "My weekend's not totally full yet."

"I'm not sure whether to be insulted or not."

She laughed. "You shouldn't be. You're cute."

He looked bemused. "You're not very shy, are you?"

"I tried being shy once, when I was three," Lucy informed him. "I figured it had to be fun, or else people wouldn't do it. It was boring, so I ditched it."

Not Quite Aware

He snorted with laughter. "You do realize people aren't shy because they choose to be, right?"

"Well, I know that *now*," Lucy said, tossing her hair. "Seriously, people would have way more fun if they weren't afraid of what other people think. Anyway, what time and place?"

"Friday night?" Pablo hazarded.

"Sure, as long as it's not immediately after school. I have another date then."

"You just . . . come right out and say that, do you?"

"I'm cute. I have dates. We're talking about scheduling here. I should be done by five, so maybe we could get together around five thirty or six?"

"Yes, your majesty," he said with a mock bow.

"Oh, yeah, and just so you know, me sitting in the bleachers watching you play basketball because you forgot you had practice that day is *not* a date," Lucy added, shaking her finger.

"That seems . . . oddly specific."

Lucy tossed her hair. "It's from personal experience."

"I would never have guessed."

"Here's my address, so you can pick me up," Lucy said. She rummaged through her purse for a pen, then grabbed his hand and wrote her address and phone number on it.

"I have a notebook," he said.

"It was an excuse to hold your hand," she said teasingly. "See you on Friday!"

And then she bounced off to the lunch line.

Right after the last bell rang, Lucy was gathering up her books and sneaking glances at Jonas, the guy she'd had a giant crush on in elementary school and who still hadn't seemed to notice she was alive, despite the fact that it was ten years later and she was now the cutest girl in the school. It was maddening that he sat next to her in the most boring class ever, and yet had never relieved her boredom by picking up on one of her flirtatious winks. Such a dunce. But so cute, anyway.

Jonas actually looked up and noticed her, for once.

"You're . . . Lucy, right?" he asked slowly.

"Yup!" she said, pleased.

He stared at her for a long moment.

She decided to help him out. "I'm free on Saturday. Just so you know."

Relief raced across Jonas's face, closely followed by panic. "Um, do you . . . would you . . . that is . . ."

Lucy waited for him to finish.

He mumbled something unintelligible.

"I'd love to go out with you," Lucy told him, hoping she was guessing what he'd said correctly. "What time?"

"One o'clock?" he hazarded.

"Sure. Okay. Looking forward to it. Bye, Jonas!"

Lucy waved and gathered up her books, and left the math classroom with a bounce in her step.

♍

After the bus arrived at her stop, Lucy hopped off and waved goodbye to the driver. "Bye, Guster!"

"Bye, Lucy!" he said, waving.

She skipped up the front steps and let herself in with a key.

To her surprise, her mom seemed to be home from work early, and she was yelling at someone on the phone in the kitchen.

"That's *not* what I said, Alfie!" her voice traveled.

Oh. Uncle Alfie. Lucy shrugged and tossed her backpack on the floor. If she was yelling at him, he deserved it.

"Lucy?" her mother called from the kitchen. "Is that you?"

"Yeah!"

"Talk to your father!" her mom shouted. "We've got some really bad news!"

Bemused, Lucy headed to her father's study. Her mom always made her dad break bad news, and it was never anything all that important. What was it this time? Had they forgotten to make dinner reservations for their date this weekend? Had one of her teachers called about her bad grades? Had her mom's favorite soap opera gotten canceled?

That would be a drag, actually. She liked the show, too.

Not Quite Aware

Lucy opened the door and strolled in. Her father was sitting at his desk, typing. When he heard the sound of the door, he turned around and looked at her. His face was very solemn.

"Who died?" Lucy asked flippantly.

"Aunt Aggie," he said.

Whoa. Someone actually had died.

For a heartbeat, Lucy thought, *Well, we barely knew her, anyway.* And then the world came crashing down around her as she remembered what this death meant.

If Aunt Aggie was dead, that meant she was cursed.

That meant she was Virgo.

Chapter 2
Not Quite a Name

"**I**'m cursed," Lucy tried saying, but the words wouldn't come. Horribly, that confirmed it.

"I'm sorry, Lucy," her father said. "That means you're Virgo."

"I know," Lucy snapped. "Did you think I couldn't figure that out? I'm not stupid."

Aunt Aggie hadn't had any kids. She'd been too much of a workaholic to even date. And her parents, siblings, and other nieces and nephews had all been born during the safe eleven-twelfths of the year. That meant Lucy had been her closest living relative born within the dangerous dates, and thus her heir to the curse.

One day, Lucy thought sourly. *One lousy day.*

If she'd been born on September 23 instead of September 22, she would have been safe. But no, she'd had the bad luck to be born two months early, just in time to inherit the Virgo curse. She'd been dreading it for most of her life, so she was used to the idea by now, but it still stank.

"We thought Aunt Aggie would live longer," Lucy's dad said. "She'd only been cursed for nine years."

Not Quite a Name

"Wha— really?" Lucy goggled at him. She'd thought she'd be able to count on a lot longer than that. "What'd she do wrong?"

Lucy's father sighed. "I don't think she bothered to fight it after the first few years. The more you let it change you, the harder it'll be to fight, after all."

Lucy's heart clenched. That was the worst thing about the curse — even worse than dying. It tried to turn your personality into the ideal Virgo. Oh, and once it succeeded, you died. Talk about a double whammy.

"I'll fight it," Lucy assured him.

"Will you?" her father asked sadly.

"Of course I will!" Lucy snapped. How could he even doubt it? "I don't want to be anything like Aunt Aggie. Talk about a boring person!"

Her father started to say something, and then stopped.

"Well," he said at last, "you hold on to that feeling. You're going to need it."

Lucy shuddered. Something creepy was going to start messing with her mind soon. What would it feel like?

She would just as soon never know, if it meant she'd never have to experience it. Too bad that was no longer an option.

"She was selfish," Lucy said angrily. "She should've hung on longer. If she had, I wouldn't have been —" She couldn't say the word. Boy, she hated this curse. "This wouldn't have happened so early!" she finished finally.

"Well . . . she probably was selfish," Lucy's father said slowly. "Selflessness was never one of Aggie's defining traits. But you have no idea how hard she struggled at first. I hope you'll find it easier to resist the curse than she did, but in case you don't . . ." He hesitated. "Well, I hope you won't judge her too harshly."

Lucy felt irrationally angry at first. But she breathed in deeply and let it go. She'd never been one for big, emotional displays.

Hurray, I get to die young, Lucy thought sourly. *Lucky me! But at least there's one thing that won't be so bad . . .*

"Do you know what my —" Lucy started to say, but she couldn't. The curse wouldn't let her.

"Do you mean your power?" her dad asked.

Lucy nodded, relieved. Maybe not being able to talk about the curse wouldn't be so bad. Her parents knew all about it, after all. They'd been the ones to tell her about it.

"I don't know," her father said. "From what I hear, every cursed person has a different power. Your aunt could magically sort data. She used it all the time as a computer programmer."

Lucy made a face. *That figures. Boring person, boring power.*

She hoped she wouldn't get something so lame that a computer could easily do it for her. She wanted a power that was so amazing, it would almost make up for the fact that she was going to die within twenty years.

Man. She was going to die within twenty years.

Stupid curse.

"Okay," Lucy said, trying to sound in control, even though it felt like her whole world was tilting sideways. "So what do we do now?"

"Well," Lucy's father said, "your mother is warning her brother."

Lucy made a face. "How is that going?"

"He still doesn't believe that curses exist."

Moron. Lucy rolled her eyes. At least she didn't have to feel too bad about her heir who would inherit the curse from her. She couldn't stand the man.

Of course, she couldn't completely blame him. Lucy's father and his sister were the ones who'd grown up in a family who'd had eight cursed Virgos in four generations. Lucy's mother and her brother hadn't. But because Lucy's nearest blood relative who'd been born between August 23 and September 22 was on her mother's side, the curse was going to skip families next time it moved on. Lucky, lucky Uncle Alfie.

Apparently the curse skipped families a lot. The bloodline of whoever-was-the-first-Virgo didn't matter, only the nearest living blood relative to whoever-was-currently-Virgo, so it often hopped from one side of a person's family to the other.

All the zodiac curses did that. That was why nobody knew when the curses had started, or why, or how.

Not Quite a Name

She didn't even know if her father's family had been from the original bloodline. Probably not.

Probably none of the families were.

"Who are the other —?" Lucy tried to ask.

"The other cursed?" her father asked.

Lucy nodded.

"I only know two of them," her dad said. "Sagittarius and Aries. I'll call them up tonight. I just wanted to tell you first."

"We're not related to them, are we?" Lucy asked cautiously. Her older sister, who was in college, had the zodiac sign of Aries.

"Oh, certainly not!" her father exploded. "I cannot understand for the life of me why two people from cursed families would ever marry! Talk about dangerous for your kids!"

"Has it happened before?" Lucy asked.

Her father nodded. "Aggie mentioned that the Aquarius and the Sagittarius married a few generations ago."

The Sagittarius. Lucy swallowed. She realized that people were going to start referring to her that way now. *The Virgo.*

That wasn't who she wanted to be. That wasn't who she *was.* As if it wasn't enough that the curse wanted to strip her of her life, her mind, her identity, it was already trying to strip away her name.

It wasn't okay. And she decided right then and there that she would never call anybody by one of those titles, no matter how convenient it might be. When she met the others, the first thing she would do was ask their names.

"Yeah, call them tonight," Lucy nodded. "We should set something up so I can meet them. As soon as possible, I guess. Oh, but not this Friday or Saturday, if those are the only times they have available," she added quickly. "I have dates."

Her dad stared at her. "Don't you think those could wait?"

"No," Lucy said. "Changing my plans is like saying this has my permission to change my life. It does not have my permission. I'm not changing my plans."

Her father looked like he was unsure whether he should be amused or relieved or exasperated. "Well . . . I'll find out when a good time for you to meet the others is, then."

"Good." Lucy nodded.

She marched towards the door and opened it. From the kitchen, she heard her mother shouting.

"Alfie! I'm telling you this because I care whether you live or die! Even though you apparently don't!"

"Uncle Alfie's going to be really surprised if he inherits the — thing — and he still doesn't believe in it," Lucy commented.

Lucy's father winced. "I hope it'll be a long, long time before that happens."

That seemed like an odd level of concern for Uncle Alfie. "Why? Because Mom would be sad?"

Her father just stared at her.

"What?"

Her father looked incredulous.

"*What?*" Lucy asked.

"Lucy," her father said, "do you honestly think I'm concerned about your mom's idiot brother?"

Oh. The obvious came crashing down on her. *Uncle Alfie won't inherit the curse until I'm dead.*

"Yes, let's spare Uncle Alfie for awhile," Lucy said lightly.

Chapter 3

Not Quite Concerned

School was a relief, because her mother's way of reacting to the bad news had turned out to be exasperating.

Her mom had spent all night making Lucy take personality tests and fill out notecards. Color-coded notecards. All about her current personality, so that she could compare herself to those notecards and tests on a regular basis and make sure the curse hadn't changed her without her noticing it.

"My personality objects to color-coded notecards," Lucy tried complaining. But her mom ignored that.

"Lucy, do you have any plans this weekend?" her dad yelled from the study at one point.

"Yeah, I told you I have dates!" she called back. "Two on Friday and one on Saturday!"

"Three dates?!" he hollered.

"Don't worry!" she called. "They're all cute!"

"And this should make me *not* worry?!"

"Sure! Wouldn't you worry more if I had such bad taste that I was going out with ugly boys instead?" Lucy called.

"No, not really!"

"Let's use a different color to symbolize a different feeling on each subject," Lucy's mother said, opening a drawer to pull out a package of twelve matching pens in various colors. "Then it will be easy to cross-reference each of the basic cards with all of the details on the white cards about specific subjects."

Lucy stared at the stack of notecards on the table. It had multiplied. They were like rabbits.

"Lucy, I'm going to set up the meeting for Saturday morning!" her father called. "Don't make any more plans during that time!"

"Got it!" she yelled back.

"And are any of those dates with young men I haven't met before?" he called.

Lucy made a face. She'd known he was going to ask that. "You've met George!"

"Then I'd better meet the other two before you go anywhere with them!"

Lucy groaned. She hated it when he met her dates.

"Now, first of all," her mother said briskly, pulling out a stack of notecards and tapping them against the table to make sure they were perfectly aligned, "what are your opinions on each of your subjects at school?"

"Blah, bleh, blug, and blarg," Lucy said promptly.

"Be serious," her mother admonished. "This information might save your life someday. We need to know exactly every nuance of your real personality."

Lucy sighed. *And taking things seriously DOESN'T go against my real personality?*

Reluctantly, she let her mother grill her, even when some of the questions were embarrassingly personal. Since psychoanalyzing herself in exhaustive detail was something Lucy never did, it wasn't long before she was squirming. But her mom just kept on going, asking more details and writing it all down in tiny, neat writing across notecard after notecard.

"Can we please do something else now?" Lucy pleaded. "I have math homework, you know!"

Not Quite Concerned

"You never finish it, anyway," her mother said flatly. She raised her voice and called, "Harry, would you find a Myers-Briggs test online and print it out for me?"

"Sure!" her father called from the study.

"Oh, could you also print me out a more detailed description of Virgo?" Lucy's mother added. "All I've got right now is *Logical, responsible, loyal, detail-oriented, shy, and deeply perfectionistic.* I'm sure there are other more subtle traits worth tracking, and I've got plenty of notecards."

"I'll print out several different descriptions!" her dad called.

Lucy put her head in her arms and moaned.

Overall, the whole night was an ordeal, and she was very, very glad to go to school the next morning.

She waved hello to everybody she met, she got asked out on another date by a guy named Evan she'd gone out with a few times, and she told him that he'd have to wait till next week to try again, because she was booked this weekend and she never planned things out more than a week in advance.

Maybe I should have told some of my friends about the curse I was going to get before it happened, Lucy thought. *They could have helped me keep an eye out for any personality changes.*

But that sounded icky-sticky touchy-feely, exactly the sort of thing Lucy hated. She didn't have friends so that she could sit around overanalyzing everything and angsting. She had friends so that they could hang out and have fun.

Nah, I don't want them to know, Lucy decided. *If they knew, they'd treat me differently. What I need is for everything to stay exactly the same.*

Which meant no stupid notecards. Seriously.

Ivan asked her out after school, and she told him the same thing she'd told Evan: to try again next week when her schedule wasn't totally full.

After school, she hung out with Carrie, Matilda, Jezza, and Natasia, accepted a ride home from Matilda who had just gotten her driver's license, and then arrived home two hours late without remembering to call her parents to let them know.

"You might have called!" her dad yelled. "We were worried!"

"Well, at least that shows I haven't changed," Lucy said pertly. "You wouldn't want me to suddenly go responsible, would you?"

That shut her father up quickly.

Lucy grinned as she skipped up the stairs two at a time. This might not be so bad, after all. Being flighty and irresponsible was the opposite of Virgo, which was exactly what her parents wanted for her. The less responsible she was, the longer she'd live! This was great!

She couldn't believe she'd missed such an obvious solution. All she had to do was behave in exactly the opposite way the ideal Virgo would.

Lucy grabbed her backpack and yanked out her just-barely-started math homework. She tore it into little shreds and scattered them around the room as confetti.

"Fly, homework! Fly!" she cried, and giggled.

Her mother knocked on her door. "Lucy, may I come in?"

"If you want!" Lucy called. "I don't care!"

Her mother came in, looking cautious. "Lucy, we need to talk."

"I don't want to talk," Lucy said, scooping up a sock from the floor. She lay back on her bed and tossed it up and down, catching it. "I'm never going to take anything seriously again."

Her mother sighed. "I was afraid you'd say something like that. Luce, you can't use your curse as an excuse for bad behavior."

"Can so," Lucy said.

"Cannot."

"Can so! You want me to stay alive longer, don't you?"

"Can I be frank?" her mother asked.

"Sure." Lucy tossed the sock in the air.

"No."

Lucy dropped the sock. She jerked up to a sitting position.

"No?" she asked, outraged.

"No," her mother said. "Not at the cost of you turning your life into something not worth living. It's possible to ruin your life in ways other than surrendering to a curse."

Lucy set her jaw.

Not Quite Concerned

"The solution isn't to abandon your self-control entirely, Lucy," her mother said. "You need to use it *more*. That's what you'll need to grow into a better version of yourself. It's also what you'll need to resist the curse."

Lucy gave her a furious look.

"I know you're scared," her mother began.

"I'm not scared!" Lucy snapped.

"Well, you should be."

Lucy realized with horror that she had a lump in her throat. She fought it back. She hated crying. It was messy and disgusting.

"So what exactly do you want me to do?" she asked rudely.

Her mom reached out and gave her a hug. "Remember who you are."

Thanks, Mom, Lucy thought sourly. *Here I was planning on completely forgetting.*

Chapter 4
Not Quite Polite

Friday took forever to come, and even after it did, it felt like the school day dragged on twice as long as usual. But when, at last, the final bell rang, Lucy exploded out of her seat and raced towards the door, joining her friend Jezza in shouting, "FREEDOM!"

The math teacher did not look pleased.

George met her at her locker while she was putting her books away.

"You ready to go get pizza?" he asked.

"Sure!" Lucy said. She dumped the rest of her backpack's contents into her locker. There was homework in there somewhere, but eh. She wasn't freaking out as much now about the curse's certainty of affecting her, but she hadn't bothered to do her homework at all since Monday, either. She'd tried a few times, but every time she'd looked at it, she'd thought, *Aunt Aggie was a workaholic,* and then she hadn't been able to stand the sight of it.

The fact of the matter was, the curse was definitely going to affect her and kill her eventually. No one had ever lasted longer than twenty years. But that didn't mean she had to help it.

Not Quite Polite

If she was going to turn into a — gag, gag — workaholic at some point in the future, she might as well enjoy her life now, while she was still herself. Future-her would probably be furious about that, but what did she care? Future-her wouldn't really be Lucy. Future-her would be Virgo.

Ugh. The future was depressing. Lucy wrenched her thoughts back to today, when she had two bright, shiny, exciting dates waiting.

"Are we doubling with one of your friends?" he asked.

"Yup," Lucy said. "Carrie and her boyfriend will meet us there."

Caleb was a new boyfriend, one Lucy had never met before. Apparently he went to a different school. Carrie tended to commit to relationships with lightning speed, and then she was just as quick about falling out of love with the guys and dumping them.

Which wasn't to say that Carrie never got dumped. She did, about a third of the time. When that happened, she'd cry for a day and eat a whole gallon of ice cream, and then she'd latch onto the nearest cute guy who asked her out and declare him her new boyfriend. It was a cycle that happened over and over again. Lucy'd learned to be skeptical whenever her friend declared she was in love.

Still, that was exactly the reason Carrie was such a great friend to go on a double date with. She almost always had a boyfriend, so it wasn't hard for her to get a date on a moment's notice, and he was almost always brand new. No pressure, in other words. That wasn't always true for Jezza or Matilda.

Worst of all was Natasia. Lucy'd tried double dating with Natasia before, but she and her boyfriend Sean had been going out for over a year, and ugh . . . those two were always holding hands or smooching or whispering in each other's ears or just generally being really uncomfortable to sit near.

So they ambled out of the school building, strolled half a block to Dave's Pizza Buffet, and Lucy waved and said hi to a dozen classmates. Finally, she noticed Carrie and a super cute guy with brown skin sitting in a booth near the back, already having helped themselves to two slices of cheap and low-quality pizza.

He's hot, Lucy thought impishly. *I'll have to see if I can get his number after Carrie dumps him.*

She and George each grabbed a plate and a slice of pizza. Then they headed over to the booth near the back.

"Hi, Caleb!" Lucy said cheerfully. "I assume you're Caleb. This is George, and I'm Lucy."

"Yo," George said.

Caleb's mouth was full, so he flicked a hand in what might have been a wave.

"We're Carrie's friends from school," Lucy said, settling into the other side of the booth. George sat beside her. "What school do you go to?"

"Freedom Prep," Caleb said, making a face. "It's a private school. My dad's really into the whole academics thing."

"And you're not?" George asked.

Carrie's new boyfriend shrugged. "I like sports better."

"And he's amazing at wrestling!" Carrie exclaimed, gazing at him with a besotted look on her face. "That's how we met!"

"That's how you *met?*" George asked, looking unsure whether to be confused or horrified.

"He beat Aaron," Carrie said, giggling. "That was back when I was dating Aaron. I'm not anymore, of course."

Lucy snatched a napkin out of the dispenser and stifled her snorts of laughter in it. That was typical Carrie. She got really into competitive sports, and she only liked winners. If a guy she was dating lost, she usually dumped him and went after someone from the opposing team.

George looked more confused than ever.

"How about you?" Carrie asked flirtatiously, leaning forward. "Do you play any sports?"

"I'm in the chess club. Does that count?" George asked.

Carrie leaned back in horror.

Lucy couldn't stifle it with her napkin any longer. She erupted into gales of laughter.

Carrie stared at her furiously.

"I need to use the bathroom," Carrie announced.

Lucy ignored the summons, blowing her nose in the napkin and going back to laughing.

"You need to use it, too," Carrie hinted threateningly.

So Lucy got up to follow her, rolling her eyes at both boys while her friend's back was turned. Caleb burst into a wide grin.

As soon as they entered the ladies' room, both girls started talking at once.

"The chess club? Are you kidding me?!"

"Could you be more transparent, Carrie?"

"The chess club!"

"George is cute, and he's nice. What's your damage?"

"That's, like, the ultimate nerd thing, Lucy!"

"Yeah, and? He can be smart if he wants. It doesn't make him a bad date. It kind of makes him the opposite."

Carrie screwed up her face. "I didn't realize you had such terrible taste in guys."

I didn't realize I had such terrible taste in friends, Lucy thought about retorting. Carrie had always amused her before, but now the girl was ticking her off.

"He's *cute,*" Lucy repeated. She barely managed to keep from snapping it. "And he's nice. And might I add that he's not your date, he's *mine?*"

Carrie sighed heavily. "That's true." Then she brightened. "What do you think of Caleb? He's gorgeous, right?"

"Totally," Lucy agreed.

"I think he's the one!" Carrie said, giggling.

"No way!" Lucy squealed, not believing a word of it.

Carrie patted her hair, checking the mirror to make sure her makeup was still perfect. She pulled a little bag from her pocket and a tiny pencil from there. She started touching up her eyeliner. "He's totally in love with me, you know, Luce. It's, like, a match made in heaven."

Lucy had heard those words a dozen times. She was starting to get sick of them.

"I'm happy for you," she said cautiously, carefully suppressing rolling her eyes.

"You don't believe me," Carrie accused. "Don't be sarcastic! That's rude!"

And dissing my date was the polite thing to do? Lucy wanted to sneer.

"I wasn't being sarcastic," Lucy said out loud. "I really am happy for you." She tried really hard to sound sincere.

"Okay, fine," Carrie said huffily, shoving the eyeliner pencil back into her makeup bag. She stuffed it in her pocket. "Let's go back to the boys."

Lucy followed her back to the dining area, feeling rather irritated. What was wrong with Carrie? She was usually so fun to be around, but today she just seemed like an annoying twit.

Chapter 5
Not Quite a Friend

Carrie was in a snippy mood for the next few minutes after they got back to the boys, but she soon got over it, and went back to behaving like her usual self. If this was her usual self.

Was Carrie always so loud and desperate for attention? Lucy wondered.

It was unsettling.

No, make that terrifying.

Because what if the curse was making her see Carrie that way?

Had the curse already changed her enough to look at everyone she knew differently? Would she start hating all of her friends? She liked her friends. She didn't want to hate them. They didn't deserve that, and she didn't deserve that kind of loneliness.

"Earth to Lucy!" Carrie said, snapping two fingers in front of her face.

Lucy snapped to attention. "What?"

"I *said,* what's your least favorite subject at school?"

That was easy. "Math," Lucy said promptly.

"Mine's English," Carrie said.

"Mine's P.E.," George put in.

"Art," Caleb said. "Mom made me take that. I'm ditching it next year."

"Okay, now, what's your *favorite?*" Carrie asked, looking around the table and pointing at Lucy.

"Music," Lucy said. That was her elective this year. "Yours?"

"Lunch!" Carrie said, and giggled as if she'd said something really clever.

"Mine's math," said George.

"Mine, too!" Caleb cried, giving him a high five.

Carrie stared at her new boyfriend with a look on her face that suggested she had just swallowed a sour lemon.

"I kind of love statistics," Caleb said. "I might major in that in college. I like stuff that's really useful, you know?"

"Oh, it's all about the theoreticals for me," George said, shaking his head. "Seriously, did you know there are an infinite number of sizes of infinity? Blows my mind!"

"Okay, what's your favorite sport?" Carrie broke in desperately.

For once, Lucy found herself in full agreement with her friend. The last thing she wanted was a conversation about math for the next half hour.

"To play, or to watch?" Caleb asked.

"Both."

"To play . . . wrestling, obviously. To watch . . . baseball."

"How about you?" Carrie asked, pointing at George.

"Do videogames count?" he hedged.

Carrie's expression said they didn't.

"Then none."

"You have to pick something."

"Who said?"

"I did!"

"But I don't like any of them. I like games that require thinking, not games where there are no brains at all."

Lucy inched away from her date.

"No brains!" Carrie exploded. "*No brains?!*"

"Okay," George said quickly, "maybe that wasn't the best —"

Not Quite a Friend

But it was too late. Carrie was already going on a loud and emphatic rant, pounding the table in several places and drowning out any attempts to stop her.

"Hey, do you all go to the same school?" Caleb broke in suddenly, talking at twice the volume Carrie was managing.

Carrie stopped, looking taken aback.

"Yes," Lucy said quickly, talking slightly louder than usual.

"Yeah," George said, looking grateful for the change of topic.

Carrie took a breath, opened her mouth . . .

"Have you two been going out long?" Caleb added.

"I wish," George said with a wry laugh. "But Lucy is, like, pathologically non-exclusive."

"Don't you think maybe calling me pathological might be a bad move?" Lucy demanded with mock offense.

George mimed holding his hands over his head.

"Anyway, like I was —" Carrie began.

"How'd you two meet, anyway?" Caleb asked.

"Let's see," George said. "I think it was that math test she needed help with at the end of last year. The teacher told her if she didn't pass it, she'd fail the class and have to make it up with summer school. She got a C, by the way, which meant she just barely passed it."

Lucy moaned. "Did you have to tell him all the details?"

"You worked hard! You should be proud!"

"No, I should be embarrassed!"

"Awwwww, but you're cute when you're embarrassed," George said, grinning.

"I'm going to get more pizza," Carrie said sulkily, sliding out of the booth and taking her empty plate with her. "Anybody else want something?"

"Hawaiian," said George.

"Pepperoni," Caleb added.

"The barbecue ranch one."

Carrie stalked off towards the pizza buffet table. There was a rather long line at the end, since the room had filled up with lots of fellow students from school.

Caleb leaned forward quickly. "Hey, I know this is awkward and bad timing and stuff, but can I get your number?"

Lucy stared at him, dumbfounded. "What?"

"Hope you don't mind," Caleb added, looking at George.

He rolled his eyes. "Whatever. I knew you were going to ask."

"Well?" Caleb asked.

"Carrie!" Lucy sputtered.

"Yeah, what about her?" Caleb asked.

"You're her *boyfriend!*"

Caleb looked baffled. "Since when? This is our first date."

Lucy stared at him in consternation. *How often does Carrie start calling guys her boyfriend on the first date? That would explain a lot about her relationships . . .*

She shook her head. No, no. It didn't matter. Carrie was her friend. You had to be loyal to your friends.

"I'm sorry," she said in a low voice. "As long as you're dating Carrie —"

"Okay, I'll break up with her right now."

Caleb hopped up and walked towards the buffet line.

"Get back here!" Lucy cried in horror.

George snorted with laughter.

Lucy gave him a furious glare and jumped up, but he didn't help her by moving out of the way, so that left her mostly trapped in the booth. She tried to edge past his knees at a snail's pace.

"It might be better if you leave them alone," George suggested. "If you jump right in the middle of that . . ."

Lucy broke free of the booth and ran towards the buffet line, but she was too late. Or rather, she was just in time to see Carrie burst into sobs and collapse to the floor, empty plate clattering beside her.

Lucy stopped, frozen. This was the worst thing that could have happened on a double date.

Then Caleb made it worse.

"Can I get your number now?" he called to Lucy.

A few girls standing in line gave Lucy shocked and outraged glares, while a few guys whistled.

Not Quite a Friend

"No!" Lucy exploded. "No, you cannot get my number! What is *wrong* with you?"

From the floor, Carrie's head lifted and gave her a hateful look.

Lucy had the sinking feeling she had just lost a friend.

Chapter 6
Not Quite Escape

After that fiasco, Lucy still had another date to get through. Two dates in one day no longer seemed quite as fun as it had a few days ago. And she still had to find a way to get home so that she could change her clothes and meet Pablo there.

George, it turned out, did not have a car. Lucy didn't have her own car, either; she sometimes borrowed one of her parents', but she hadn't done that today. Under normal circumstances, this wouldn't have been a problem, since she could have just asked Carrie to drop her off at home in her ancient clunker that she was so proud of. But that . . . obviously wasn't going to happen today.

So she had to endure the ultimate humiliation: calling her parents to ask them to pick her up.

Her dad was the one who drove to get her. When she got in the car, he asked, "So what was wrong with Carrie? Your mother said you said there was some reason she couldn't drop you off at home."

Lucy groaned and buckled her seat belt. "It's a totally long story."

Not Quite Escape

"I'm a totally curious person, and this car doesn't have to go anywhere. We could just sit here for hours while I wait to hear what happened . . ."

Lucy glared at her father for this transparent ploy to get her to talk about her personal life, but whatever. It wasn't like the story wouldn't end up all over the school by tomorrow, anyway. Practically half the school had been there watching.

"Carrie's boyfriend hit on me," Lucy said sulkily. "She totally hates me now."

"Did you apologize?"

"It's not my fault!" Lucy cried. "I didn't encourage him! In fact, I told him no way would I ever date him as long he was dating Carrie, and then he went and broke up with her!"

Lucy's father started snickering.

"It's not funny!"

He straightened his face with great effort. "Right. You're right. Of course not. Please continue."

Lucy sighed and slouched back against the seat. "That's it."

"Really?" her father said. "That doesn't seem like that long of a story. I was looking forward to a long story."

"It *felt* long!"

"Right." Her father nodded seriously. "Just like every time I have to watch you go out the door with another young man I've never seen before in my life, and then I spend my whole evening worrying. Speaking of which, who is tonight's model?"

"Pablo," Lucy said. "His name is Pablo."

"Is he cute?"

"Why would you care?"

"Just taking an interest."

"Well, don't. It sounds weird."

Her dad tried very hard to keep a straight face.

"Daaaad," Lucy complained. "Can we go home now, please? I need to touch up my makeup, and I want to change my outfit."

He glanced at her. "What's wrong with what you're wearing?"

"Nothing's *wrong* with it," Lucy said impatiently. "It's just that he saw me wearing this outfit at school."

"And . . .?"

"And I don't want him to think I'm the sort of person who wears the same thing, like, all the time!"

"Heaven forbid," her father said dryly, looking down at his army uniform.

"Exactly! Oh, and if you try to scare him off by showing up at the door polishing a shotgun or something, then —" She shook her finger.

"Then what?" her father asked with interest.

"Then *hmph!*" She stuck out her tongue at him.

Lucy's dad grinned and started the car.

At last, they were heading home. As soon as the car stopped, Lucy flung her door open and bolted for the house. She had only forty-five minutes left before Pablo arrived, and she didn't want to be late and give her father more time to interrogate him. That would be the end of the world.

She kept a close eye on the clock as she decided what to wear, calculating in her head how long it would take to get ready so that she knew how long she had to choose the perfect outfit. After trying on four and discarding three, she kept a long purple blouse and a super cute denim skirt she'd bought with her last allowance. Then she loaded up her arms with dozens and dozens of bracelets that jangled while she moved. She liked the way the noise made her the center of attention when she wore them.

Lucy was just giving her ponytail one last spritz of hairspray when the doorbell rang.

"I'll get it!" she cried, tossing the bottle on the counter of the bathroom. It rolled and fell to the ground, but she didn't stop to pick it up. She just raced downstairs.

Have to get to the door before Dad . . . have to get to the door before Dad . . .

"Hello," her father's voice said. "You must be Pablo."

Argh! Lucy let out a silent scream as she jumped down the last few steps and bolted for the front door.

"Gee, thank you for coming, Pablo!" she said brightly. "You have reservations that we can't be late for, right? Right. Let's go!"

Pablo looked confused. "I don't —"

"Now, Lucy, you know how this works," her father said, clapping Pablo on the shoulder rather harder than necessary. "I'm Lucy's father. You can call me 'sir.' Before you take my daughter anywhere, there are some ground rules you need to know . . ."

And thus began the usual torturous, embarrassing ordeal that Lucy had desperately wanted to skip. She practically had the whole speech memorized, so she wandered over to the kitchen, where her mom was busy filling in a spreadsheet on her laptop.

"Dad's giving one of my dates 'the talk' again," Lucy complained. "Can't he lay off, for once?"

Lucy's mom didn't even look up from her laptop. "Given that your cousin got pregnant in high school, no, I don't think so."

Lucy made a face.

"I've been typing up your notecards," Lucy's mom said, glancing up and tapping the side of the screen. "Want to see?"

Lucy wavered. On the one hand, it sounded kind of interesting, but on the other hand, yuck.

Her mom turned the laptop so that Lucy could see the screen better. It was a color-coded masterpiece of perfectionism. Lucy instinctively, passionately loathed it.

"Gee," she said, trying to think of something that wasn't, *That's even worse than the notecards.*

"I'm working on a scoring rubric," her mom said. "That way, you can take a test every week, and we'll be able to quantitatively compare your scores with where they used to be —"

"Oh, I think Dad's wrapping up now! Gotta go!" Lucy cried.

She raced back to the living room just in time to catch the tail end of her dad's speech. Anything was better than agreeing to take extra tests every week. Talk about a curse, sheesh.

"Now, one last thing," Lucy's father was saying. "I may not own a shotgun, but I want you to know that I do own . . . *this.* And I know how to use it."

He seized a well-thumbed volume from the bookcase and held it up intimidatingly.

Lucy groaned. Was he trying to humiliate her?

When at last the interminable lecture was over, Lucy went out to her date's car. Pablo held the door open for her, and glanced back at the front door where her dad was watching. Her father nodded curtly. Then Pablo got in the driver's seat.

"Sorry about my dad," Lucy said, shaking her head. "He is way overprotective. Talk about annoying."

As he turned the key into the ignition, Pablo remarked, "You know, I think the fact that your dad owns Sun Tzu's *Art of War* and knows how to use it is a lot more intimidating than a shotgun would be."

Chapter 7
Not Quite a Shock

Despite her dad's attempt to ruin the date by making her die of embarrassment before it started, the date went very well after that.

They went to see a horror flick, they smuggled hot dogs into the theater and bought a giant tub of popcorn, they wound up throwing most of the popcorn at each other, and they walked out of the building cracking up as they made fun of the characters, who had been way too stupid to live.

She had such a good time that when he said goodbye to her at the door, she spontaneously leaned over and kissed him.

He blinked as she pulled back. "I thought you told me you didn't kiss on the first date."

She smirked. "Only if I make the first move."

At that point, the door flew open, and her father stood there with a gigantic scowl.

"Bye, Pablo!" Lucy said, ducking under her father's arm to get in the house.

"See you at school on Monday!" he called.

Her father shut the door and folded his arms.

"It's none of your beeswax who I kiss, Dad," Lucy said.

"Didn't you just meet him a few days ago?"

"Yeah. And I like him."

"Don't you have another date tomorrow?"

"Yep, and I like him, too."

Her father glowered.

Lucy proceeded to spend the rest of the night ignoring her homework and putting sticky notes in her favorite pages of some fashion magazines she'd bought a few weeks ago. If she used sticky notes, she'd hopefully remember where to find the pages, and could take the magazines with her next time she went shopping. It was a genius plan.

Her older sister Lila called, freaking out because she'd only just checked her messages and gotten the news that Aunt Aggie had died and Lucy was cursed now.

Once Lucy assured her that things were fine, and no she had no clue what her magic power was, and yes she'd call her when she found out, the two of them wound up gabbing for hours about just about everything. It was amazing how well they got along now that they no longer lived in the same house.

"Just take care of yourself, Luce," Lila said as they were about to hang up. "I want you to stay alive."

"That's not what you used to say," Lucy said with a grin.

Lila snickered. "What can I say? College has matured me."

By the time the call ended, it was well past her usual bedtime, so Lucy brushed her teeth and headed to bed. Since it wasn't a school night and she'd been talking to Lila, they hadn't put a limit on her phone time.

Lucy lay awake for a long time, wondering.

What *was* her power? Would it be something cool? She really hoped it wouldn't have anything to do with spreadsheets.

She fell asleep and had unsettling dreams about color-coded math tests and her father throwing books at all of her dates.

♏

Not Quite a Shock

Lucy overslept the next morning, and only woke up when her father called up the stairs.

"Lucy, they're here!"

Who's here? she thought, rubbing her eyes groggily. *My date with Jonas isn't till this afternoon.*

Then she remembered, and her eyes widened. She jumped out of bed, spurred by adrenaline, and dressed with rapid haste. In only a few minutes, with no makeup and her hair unbrushed, she was running downstairs to meet the other cursed.

"They" turned out to have been an overstatement. So far there was only one person, an old man with brown skin and grey hair. He was sitting on the armchair, talking with her parents. Lucy came in, and he held out his hand. She took it gingerly.

"Hello," he beamed, shaking her head. "I'm Aaron Watson. You can call me Aaron."

"Aaron," Lucy repeated. It was odd to hear someone her grandpa's age asking her to call him by his first name, but nice. She hated calling people by their last names. It seemed so impersonal.

"I was born on March twenty-sixth," he added.

Lucy's mind went blank. She knew he was trying to tell her what his curse was, but the date meant nothing to her. The only zodiac birthdays she knew were Virgo's.

"Aries," Lucy's mom said helpfully.

"Oh!" Lucy said. "How long have you been . . . um . . ."

"Five years," he said, smiling.

"Five days," she said, pointing at herself.

"So I've heard."

There was a sound of a car driving up, and the doorbell rang a moment later. Lucy's dad got up to answer it. He came back with —

"Alex Winters?" Lucy blurted out.

He was a guy from her school. He was *the* guy, in fact, who had taken her out on a date to watch him play basketball because he had forgotten he had practice that day.

He seemed similarly surprised to see her. "You're, uh . . ."

"*Lucy,*" she said impatiently. "We've been on two dates. The least you could do is remember my name."

"Sorry," he said.

Honestly, Lucy thought, rolling her eyes. *You're not getting a third date.*

"Hi, Alex!" Aaron called from his chair, waving. "Is Xander coming today?"

"No."

"Xander?" Lucy's mom asked.

"His twin brother," Aaron said. "Which means . . ." He lowered his voice as if he were about to reveal something very significant. ". . . they were born on the same day."

"Ohhhhh," Lucy's parents said in unison.

Uh, yeah? Lucy thought. *That's what being twins means.*

"So Xander is Alex's heir," Lucy's dad said slowly. "Or is it the reverse?"

"You got it right the first time," Aaron said.

But Lucy had noticed something far more interesting. "What's Xander short for?" she demanded.

Alex sighed. "It's short for my parents not having much imagination and giving us really similar names."

"Yes, but what's it short *for?*"

"Alessandro."

"And your name is Alexander?"

"Yes, but call me Alex, please."

The boy was extremely polite and extremely distant. He sat stiffly on the sofa. Lucy found herself rather exasperated.

"Are any of the heirs coming?" Lucy's mom asked anxiously. "It will be much easier to talk about things if we have people who can, well, talk about them."

"I know Steven's bringing his son," the old man answered. "My granddaughter lives several states away, and she's only seven years old, anyway. Catherine was too busy to come today, and her nephew is in college across the country, so he won't be here, either."

"Who is which?" Lucy's father inquired.

Not Quite a Shock

"Let's see," Aaron said. "Catherine's birthday is . . . I'm trying to remember . . ."

"Late July," Alex said.

Lucy's mother thought for a moment. "Leo?"

"Yes!" the old man said, looking pleased.

"What about yours?" Lucy's mom asked, looking at Alex.

"June eighth."

"Gemini?" she hazarded.

He nodded.

"That's the sign for twins, isn't it?" she asked. "How appropriate that you actually *are* a twin!"

"Funny, I've never heard that before," he said flatly.

"So we're just waiting for the Sagittarius and his son?" Lucy's dad asked.

Lucy blinked. She'd assumed there would be a lot more people than that. "Why just —?"

There came a loud knock at the door. Since Lucy was the only one standing, she went to get it. When she opened the door, there was a middle-aged man standing there.

"Hello," he said, shaking her hand. "I'm Steven. And you are?"

"Lucy."

"So you're the one this meeting is about."

She nodded.

"Well, I'm pleased to meet you, even if the circumstances are no doubt not very pleasant for you." Steven stepped to the side. "This is my son, Caleb."

And in that moment, Lucy knew true horror.

Chapter 8
Not Quite So Good

Yes, it was him. Of course it was him. That was just the way her luck went, apparently. Not only was he standing right in front of her, she now had to converse with him.

"Hi, Caleb," Lucy said frostily.

Steven looked startled. "Have you two met?"

Lucy tossed her hair haughtily. "He broke up with my friend Carrie in order to ask *me* out yesterday."

"I was only following your suggestion!" Caleb cried.

"If you wanted to stop dating her without hurting her feelings, it wouldn't even have been that hard!" Lucy yelled. "She breaks up with any guy who loses a sports game!"

Caleb paused, looking incredulous. "Wow. Really?"

Steven's eyebrows quirked. "This sounds like an amusing story. But can we talk about it later? Caleb's the only person who'll be able to speak freely, so he needs to be here. Can we come in?"

"My parents can speak freely, too," Lucy said with ill grace, but she moved aside to let them enter.

"Hi, Alex," Caleb said, flopping on the sofa next to him.

"Hi," Alex said. "What's this about Carrie?"

"Where's Xander?" Caleb countered. "Hasn't he shown up?"

Alex sighed. "Why does everyone keep asking that? No."

"He really ought to have come," Steven said, taking a seat on the end of the sofa beside his son.

"Xander does what Xander wants to do," Alex said tightly. "I don't control him."

"He doesn't even control himself!" Caleb said, cracking up.

Alex looked mildly annoyed.

So Alex's brother is a jerk, Lucy noted. *We're probably lucky he didn't show up.*

"Okay, so," Lucy said, taking a seat cross-legged on the floor, since all the chairs were taken, "what do I need to know?"

"About what?" Caleb asked.

"About the —!" She couldn't say the word. "Well, obviously!"

"Okay, but where do you want me to start?"

Lucy gave him a frustrated stare. "If I could say specifics, I wouldn't have had to let you come in. Maybe you could explain why you guys are the only people here?"

Caleb shrugged. "The Leo's busy at work. The Pisces lives in London. The Aquarius ran away years ago. And the other five are missing."

"Missing?" Lucy repeated.

"Yep."

"What do you mean, 'missing'?"

"I mean 'missing.' We don't know who they are."

"*How?*" Lucy shouted.

"Why are they missing?" Lucy's mother exclaimed.

"How could you lose an entire cursed family?" Lucy's father asked incredulously at the same time.

"Curses jump families," Caleb said. "It's that whole 'closest living relative' thing, you know? Sometimes there's nobody closely related with the same zodiac sign."

"But even then, surely it's not *that* hard to go back a few generations and figure out who your closest living relative with the same zodiac sign is," Lucy's mother argued.

"Not every family keeps records back four or five generations, much less eight or nine," Steven said. "And sometimes . . . well . . ."

He glanced at Caleb.

"Sometimes someone's naughty and fathers an illegitimate kid nobody knows exists, including him, so the heir turns out to be someone random that can't be tracked," Caleb smirked. "Taurus and Libra were *both* lost in the sixties. Guess why."

Lucy shuddered. It was horrible to think about how many people must have died without even knowing they had a curse. In fact, the ones who didn't know probably died more quickly than the ones who *did* know, because they wouldn't even realize that they ought to resist.

"Okay!" Lucy declared, smacking her hand on the floor. She was sick of thinking gloom-and-doom stuff. "Now what about the good thing?"

"What good thing?" Caleb asked.

"The good thing!"

"What good thing?"

"The! Good! Thing!"

"I think she's talking about this," Steven said.

He waved his hands, and landscapes and cityscapes flickered wildly around them. Lucy's mouth fell open in awe.

"How does it work?" she squealed.

"I can't explain it," he said. "I can only demonstrate it."

"He can show places he wants to visit," Caleb said, looking bored. "Only places, not people. He doesn't use it much."

"Why not?" Lucy demanded. "That's awesome!"

"Because I want to live," Steven answered.

That seemed like no answer at all. Lucy was baffled.

"Because it makes Dad want to travel," Caleb said impatiently. "Which makes him more like Sagittarius. So he doesn't use it."

"That seems so unfair," Lucy said, feeling sorry for the man. "The good part just makes the bad part worse."

"Oh, grow up!" Caleb snorted. "You think the magical powers are a good thing? They're *all* like that."

"Like what?" Lucy asked, confused.

Not Quite So Good

Caleb's voice dripped with condescension. "Whatever the curse gives you is meant to tempt you into becoming more like what it wants you to be. The more you use it, the more likely you are to surrender to it. *All* the powers are like that. Using your power is a good way to die quickly."

Lucy stared at him in horror. "No — wait — *what?*"

Lucy's mother gasped. "Nobody told us —"

"Aggie never mentioned —" Lucy's father broke in.

"There's no cause for alarm," Aaron said soothingly.

Lucy leaned forward, hanging on his every word. His voice was magnetic. She instinctively trusted everything he said.

"He doesn't truly understand anything," the old man went on. "There's no risk to anybody at all."

Lucy nodded. Of course he was right. Why had she been worried?

"Knock it off, old man!" Caleb shouted.

Aaron sat back, his dark eyes twinkling. "I thought we were demonstrating what we can do for the young lady."

Lucy gasped, suddenly realizing what he meant. "Was that your — your — your thing I can't say —?"

"His power," Caleb said, folding his arms.

Aaron shrugged and smiled. "I try to avoid using mine, too. Quite apart from wanting to live, I'd rather not manipulate people against their will. It doesn't seem like a good thing to be doing."

Lucy's pulse raced, thinking of how easily that power could be misused. She was glad it seemed to belong to a relatively harmless old man, and not some wannabe dictator tyrant.

"So — so what you just said," Lucy's mother sputtered, "about there being no cause to worry — that was —"

"A lie," the old man said with an impish smile. "Listen to Caleb, not me. Especially if I sound particularly trustworthy."

Lucy whipped her head over to look at Alex. "What about you?" she demanded.

Alex looked uncomfortable. "I can't demonstrate mine."

"Can't or won't?" Lucy asked suspiciously.

"Can't," Caleb said. "He reads his brother's mind. That's his power. Stinks to be him, in my opinion."

Lucy made a face. She loved her older sister, but she'd hate to be inside her head all the time. "So you rarely use it?"

"No," Alex said. "Unfortunately."

"Some of the powers don't turn off," Caleb shrugged. "His is one of them. Lucky him, right?"

"What's your brother thinking now?" Lucy asked curiously.

"Even if I were capable of answering that question — which I'm not, for the same reason that Steven couldn't answer your question to him a minute ago — I wouldn't want to."

"Privacy?" Lucy asked.

"I really couldn't care less about his privacy," Alex said darkly. "But his thoughts should never be repeated in front of a girl."

"Lucy, you are never dating Alex's twin," her father said immediately.

"Dad," Lucy said, looking at him with exasperation, "I haven't even met that guy, okay? Quit with the overprotectiveness."

"What about you?" Caleb asked.

"What about me?" Lucy turned to look at him.

"Yeah. What's your magical power?"

"That's why I brought up the subject!" Lucy exclaimed. She looked around the room hopefully. "Do you know what it is?"

Chapter 9
Not Quite the Hope

"We have no idea," Steven said. "Have you tried testing it?"

Lucy was very annoyed. Of course she hadn't tried testing it. What did they think she was, her mother with the notecards and the color-coded spreadsheets?

"No," she said, a little rudely. "There's been nothing *to* test."

"I'm sure it'll turn up eventually," Aaron said kindly.

That was not what Lucy had wanted to hear. She'd wanted answers, not a bunch of shrugs all around. If they were going to be unhelpful, they could at least have been eye candy. Steven was her dad's age and presumably married, Aaron was ancient, Alex was boring as toast, and as for Caleb . . .

Okay, Caleb *was* eye candy. He was totally gorgeous. His dark brown skin was a delicious contrast to his white T-shirt and faded denim jacket, and the long sleeves of his jacket didn't quite conceal the fact that he was well-built. Shame about him being a jerk.

"Look, what exactly do you have against me?" Caleb burst out.

Lucy sniffed. "The fact that you treated my friend like dirt might have something to do with it."

"I'm sorry, okay? I'll apologize to her! I'll even go out with her again if you really want me to, but *you're* the one I like, not her!"

A puzzled look flickered across Alex's face.

That was delightfully flattering, and if only he hadn't met Carrie first, Lucy would have thoroughly enjoyed hearing it.

"Well, I'm sorry," Lucy said loftily. "After yesterday, I don't think I could ever go out with you, even if you got back together with Carrie and she dumped you next time. She'd never forgive me."

"Are you kidding me?!" Caleb shouted.

Lucy's mother jumped to her feet. "You know, I forgot to prepare that veggie platter that I wanted to make. I'll be right back."

"I'll help, too," Aaron said, getting up.

"And me," Steven said hastily.

Three of the adults escaped into the kitchen.

"I know we only just met, but I really want to go out with you!" Caleb cried. "It's so unfair that you won't give me a chance!"

Lucy had to admit that she was enjoying this. Just a smidge. "Nope," she said with a coy smile.

Alex rubbed his forehead.

Lucy's dad sat on his chair, folding his hands over his knees and smiling broadly.

"Harry! Come in here to help me!" Lucy's mom called.

"I'm supervising!" he called.

"Supervise from the kitchen!" she yelled.

With a grumpy look on his face, Lucy's father got up and headed out of the room.

"Do you want me to grovel?" Caleb demanded. "Is that it?"

"I don't want anything from you," Lucy said, tossing her hair. *Except to look at you, maybe,* she thought wickedly. *You're even more gorgeous when you're mad at me.*

"ARGH!" Caleb shouted.

Lucy's dad poked his head back into the living room to make sure they were still arguing, looked pleased with what he saw, and disappeared back into the kitchen.

"Please," Caleb pleaded. "I'm going crazy. I'm crazy about *you.* You have to go out with me. You have to!"

Not Quite the Hope

Lucy giggled and shook her head.

Alex muttered something under his breath.

"Do you have something to say, Gemini boy?" Caleb roared.

"Only that I think we've found the answer to Lucy's question," Alex said with faint exasperation.

Lucy's heart leapt. "You mean my —" Of course she couldn't say it, so she phrased it indirectly. "You mean, the good thing?!"

"Mmm. First of all, you've been the only thing half the guys at school have talked about for the past week. It's getting annoying, frankly."

Lucy grinned. She didn't see what that had to do with her magical power, but . . .

Caleb looked steamed.

"And second, him." Alex pointed at Caleb. "He never chases girls like this. He only dates girls who chase him."

"I do not!" Caleb said indignantly.

"Yes, you do."

"I do not!"

"You do. Now, try to think with a clear head if you're currently capable of it, and come to the logical conclusion."

Caleb looked ticked off, but his face screwed up for a moment. Then horror dawned. "Wait . . . No way."

"Yes way," Alex said.

"No way, what?" Lucy asked.

Caleb pointed at her, outraged. "*You!*" he shouted.

Now Lucy was really confused. "Me what?"

"You made me fall in love with you!"

Lucy giggled and flipped her hair. "I'm sorry, but there's just no way that we could —"

"Forget that!" Caleb exploded. "Forget all of that! That was your power! You're, like, some kind of siren!"

Lucy blinked at him. "I'm what now?"

Lucy's father poked his head into the living room again with a suspicious look. "Did I hear someone say they were in —"

"*Her!*" Caleb shouted, pointing at Lucy. "Her power is to make guys fall in love with her! I can't believe I fell for it!"

Horror darted across her father's face. "Iris?!" he yelled back to the kitchen in a panicked tone.

"That's not what it is," Lucy said, offended. "I'm just really cute. I've always been popular."

"So is Caleb," Alex said. "As far as I know, he's never begged for a date before."

Caleb folded his arms and muttered under his breath.

Lucy's mother came back into the living room. "What's up?"

Steven and Aaron followed, one holding a large bowl of dip and the other an enormous vegetable platter.

"They've figured out Lucy's power," her dad growled.

"Oh, have they?" A smile split across Aaron's wrinkled face. "Congratulations."

"They have not," Lucy said indignantly. "They've got it wrong. They're both just jealous that a whole lot of guys like me."

"What?" Lucy's mom asked, looking baffled.

"She's a siren!" Caleb accused. "She makes guys fall in love with her! Poor, defenseless guys, who have no clue that she's a vicious predator!"

Steven whistled.

"I am not!" Lucy cried.

Lucy's mother's mouth fell open. "Is that kind of power possible?"

"Very possible," Steven said. "There was a — someone born in late June who had something very like that a century ago."

"We're going to be mobbed by teenage boys," Lucy's dad said, with a hint of hysteria. "We'll never be able to get rid of them!"

Lucy's stomach twisted. What if they were right? What if that was all her magical power was?

No. She didn't want that power. That was a *terrible* power. Carrie and Matilda and Jezza would never forgive her if all their boyfriends fell for Lucy instead, not to mention Natasia's boyfriend that she'd been dating for over a year. That couldn't possibly be her power!

Wait . . . that *couldn't* possibly be her power.

"If that's the case, why weren't you affected?" Lucy demanded, pointing at Alex. "Or half the guys at school?"

Not Quite the Hope

Alex shrugged, pointing at himself and Steven and Aaron. "Those of us with circumstances like ours might be immune."

"Okay, then why not every old guy I've passed on the street? Why not every male teacher in school?"

"There could be an age limitation," Aaron suggested.

"Okay, then how about this? I've only been asked out by nine guys this week."

"*Nine?*" her father asked.

"Don't worry, I told the rest they have to wait to ask me until next week," Lucy said carelessly. "I knew this weekend was booked."

Her dad didn't look comforted.

"Anyway . . ." Lucy said, tossing her hair, "none of them were guys I've told to get lost in the past, and some of those jerks are really pushy. Explain that."

"Attraction and repulsion, maybe?" Aaron murmured.

Lucy gave him a blank look.

Understanding dawned in Lucy's mother eyes. "You mean she only attracts the guys she wants to? And makes the ones she doesn't want uninterested in her? That's a pretty amazing power. I would've killed for that in high school."

Lucy's father looked terribly disgruntled.

Her mom elbowed him in the ribs. "This is the point when you say I didn't need a power to attract you."

"There wouldn't be much point to me saying it now that you already have, would there?"

"Say it anyway!"

"You're not my superior officer. I don't take orders from you." But he planted a kiss on top of her head.

"Nice theory, but that doesn't explain what happened to me," Caleb said, folding his arms.

Lucy carefully avoided his eyes.

"Unless it *does!*" he added indignantly.

"You're cute," she said with great dignity. "I won't apologize for noticing that."

Alex's lips trembled, and he started snickering quietly.

Chapter 10
Not Quite the Fear

Knowing that there was probably a magical reason why Jonas had finally noticed her made their date that afternoon seem both more and less fun. More fun, because she'd had the biggest crush on him in elementary school, and it was satisfying to know that he liked her even more now than she'd liked him back then. Less fun, because . . . well . . . the fact that it was happening because of magic was outright disturbing.

Still! She decided there was nothing she could do about it, since her power seemed to be one of those things that didn't turn off, so she might as well enjoy it.

Well, as much as she could enjoy a hockey game, anyway. The game was pretty violent, and Jonas kept shouting with glee over it, which she totally didn't get. But the ice skating part was cool. It seemed like it would probably be fun to play.

But boyyyy, was she dreading Monday. She'd texted Carrie eight billion times over the weekend, apologizing every time, but Carrie had ignored them all. She hadn't heard from any of her other friends over the weekend, either.

Not Quite the Fear

Not that she'd had any reason to expect to hear from them, because she hadn't texted or called them, but she was still dreading to find out whether Carrie had ranted to them about the whole thing on Friday. What if they all hated her now?

Lucy walked into the school building with great trepidation.

"Hey, Luce!" Jezza called, waving. There were dozens of wooden bracelets on her arms, and they clacked together as her arm raised. "Heard about what happened on Friday!"

Lucy's heart clenched.

"Hilarious!" Jezza added, grinning. She tossed her head, which shook her wild black curls. "Don't worry about all the rumors. Those girls are just jealous."

"Thanks," Lucy said, a trifle relieved.

That's one friend I still have.

After a few minutes of idle chatting with Jezza, she saw Matilda amble past them, chatting with a hot football player named Brian. He was one of the not-a-prize guys Lucy had told to get lost in the past.

"Hey, Matty!" Jezza called, waving. "Get over here!"

"Huh?" Matilda turned around and saw them.

Lucy's shoulders stiffened as Brian looked at her, but there was no apparent interest in his eyes as he glanced past her, gave Jezza a flirtatious raise of an eyebrow, and then swaggered off, leaving the three girls alone.

"Did you hear the story about last Friday?" Jezza exclaimed.

Lucy wanted to die.

"No," Matilda said blankly.

"Lucy and Carrie went on a double date," Jezza said eagerly, "and Carrie's latest boyfriend totally fell for Lucy instead! I wish I'd been there to see it! It sounds hilarious!"

"Ugh. Poor Carrie," Matilda said, wincing.

"Eh, don't worry about her," Jezza said, waving her hand. "You know what she's like. She'll get over it in, like, two minutes."

"You're right," Matilda said, nodding slowly. "Anyway, you did that to me once before."

"Wah ha ha! Sorry!" Jezza cried.

Lucy strongly disagreed. There was no way Carrie was going to get over that situation so easily. Still, Lucy wasn't going to argue with her friends when they were acting like it had just been a joke and not a reason to be angry with her.

And then Natasia walked past, holding hands with her long-term boyfriend, Sean.

Lucy tensed. Panic lanced through her mind. *Don't think he's attractive, don't think he's attractive, don't think he's attractive . . .*

She had never even bothered to look at him that way, since he was Natasia's boyfriend. But now it felt like somebody had told her not to think of pink elephants. The more she tried, the harder it was not to do so.

She desperately tried to not notice how cute he was with the curl of hair over his ear, the dimple in his left cheek, those super long eyelashes —

ARGH ARGH ARGH ARGH!

At least the two were walking away. Lucy was going to have to avoid Sean forever. Did she have any classes with him? He was a junior and she was a sophomore, so it was possible they didn't. She'd never paid attention to that. She hoped not.

"Hey, Nat! Did you hear what happened to Lucy and Carrie?" Jezza called.

And to Lucy's horror, Natasia and Sean turned around and headed over to them.

Don't look at me, don't fall in love with me, don't look at me, don't fall in love with me! Lucy thought in frenzied terror.

"No," Natasia said, as Sean picked up her hand that he was holding and kissed it. Those two were usually ridiculously sappy, so this was typical for them. "What happened?"

"Lucy and Carrie went out on a double date, and Carrie's boyfriend fell for Lucy instead!" Jezza howled.

"Oh," Natasia said. "Well, maybe if she didn't start calling guys her boyfriends on the first date . . ."

Sean kissed the back of her neck, and she turned around and kissed him full on the lips.

Lucy groaned, as she usually did. *We're in public!*

Not Quite the Fear

"Anyway, so you'd better watch out for Lucy," Jezza teased. "She might be a boyfriend-stealer."

Lucy tensed. That wasn't something to joke about!

Sean barely flicked a gaze over at Lucy. "I've only got eyes for Natasia."

"And I've only got eyes for you," Natasia purred.

The two of them started smooching again.

Lucy stared at them in astonishment. *Then Sean wasn't . . . affected?*

Maybe she had the ability to turn her power off if she really wanted to. Or maybe she hadn't really been attracted to him. Or maybe her power didn't work on guys who were already in love with somebody else.

She hoped it was that last one. Then she'd never have to worry about stealing boyfriends. That would be a relief.

Lucy said bye to her friends and headed to her locker, feeling buoyant. Things were okay. Nothing had changed.

Carrie was waiting at her locker for her.

Lucy gulped and slowed to a halt. She didn't want to move forward. She wanted to turn and run away. But Carrie looked up at her, her gaze fixed and stern, and Lucy realized she had no choice if she wanted any chance to make up with her. Slowly, she walked forward, cringing inside at every step.

"So," Carrie said, as soon as she got there.

"Hi," Lucy said awkwardly.

"You texted me a bajillion times."

"I'm sor—"

"You *said* that."

"Yeah, I did."

They stood in silence for a moment.

"Caleb's a wuss," Carrie said. "It wasn't going to work out with us anyway."

Lucy stared at her, startled. "It wasn't?"

"I saw Alex and Caleb playing basketball near my house on Saturday," Carrie explained. "Alex *creamed* him. Can you believe that? Caleb is such a loser!"

Lucy's mouth fell open. *Does Alex want to date her? She doesn't seem like his type at all! Or wait . . . is he planning to lose to somebody else before long?*

"Alex even invited me to watch him at practice after school today," Carrie giggled. "Isn't that great? He's so cute! I can't wait until our first date!"

"Uh, y-yeah," Lucy said weakly. *That answers that question.*

"No stealing him!" Carrie declared, pointing at her fiercely.

"Never again!" Lucy said, crossing her heart. "I swear!"

"Good." Carrie hesitated for a moment. "Well, I'll see you at lunch," she said at last, and walked off.

Lucy breathed in and out, a sigh of relief.

She'd never dare go on a double date with Carrie again. That was clearly asking for trouble. In fact, double dates at all might be off the table for the foreseeable future, which was a shame. But otherwise, things could now go back to normal.

"Hey, Lucy!" Evan cried, catching sight of her and running over. "You said that we could set up a date this week, right? It's Monday."

"Oh, Lucy!" Ian cried, spying her. "It's Monday!"

"Right!" Donnie cried, running over.

Okay . . . not *completely* back to normal.

Maybe it's not quite such a curse to be Virgo, after all, Lucy thought with a mischievous smile.